Sharon and Darren

Nigel Gray and Cathy Wilcox

Collins

Look out for more *Jets* from Collins

First published by A & C Black Ltd in 1993
First published by Young Lions in 1994
and reprinted in Collins in 1995
10 9 8 7 6 5 4 3
Collins is an imprint of HarperCollins*Publishers* Ltd,
77–85 Fulham Palace Road, Hammersmith, London W6 8JB

ISBN 0 00 674879 1

Text © Nigel Gray 1993
Illustrations © Cathy Wilcox 1993

The author and the illustrator assert the moral right to
be identified as the author and the illustrator of the work.
A CIP record for this title is available from the British Library.
Printed and bound in Great Britain by
Caledonian International Book Manufacturing Ltd, Glasgow

I've got a boyfriend.
His name is Darren.
Sharon and Darren –
we make a poem.

Darren's going to buy me a
crunchy bar.

He said to wait by the corner shop
at half past three.

My dad bought me a digital watch
for my birthday.

It's 3.31.

Darren hasn't come.

It's 3.32.

Perhaps he's got a new girlfriend.

He's always talking to that Tracy-Marie.

She's not a
nice girl.

She picks
her nose when
no one's
looking

– and flicks it.

It's 3.33.

Perhaps he's been run over.
Perhaps a huge road roller was
coming down the street,

and now poor Darren's as flat as
a pancake all covered with
strawberry jam.

It's 3.34.

11

Perhaps, just as he was about to come out of the house, he needed to go to the toilet,

and perhaps he slipped in,
and got stuck,

and had to go to
the hospital with the toilet seat
stuck on his bum.

It's 3.35.

Perhaps he was walking along,
thinking about me, thinking about
us being a poem – Sharon and
Darren, not looking where he
was going,

and he fell down a great big hole
in the road, and got washed through
a slimy sewer,

and an alligator was lying in wait
in all that mucky water,

and with one mighty snap of
its great jaws it crunched poor
Darren in two, swallowed the bits,

and spat out Darren's teeth, and toe nails, and his zips.

It's 3.36.

Perhaps Darren
broke a cup
when he had
a drink

and tried to
mend it with
superglue,

and his hand
got stuck to
the cup,

and the cup got
stuck to the table,
and when he tried
to wipe the
glue off

he got some glue
on his other hand,
and his nose
started itching, and
he scratched it,

and his other
hand got stuck
to his nose,

and he dropped some
glue on the floor,

SPLOOT

and one foot
got stuck to
the carpet,

and the dog
came along
to sniff Darren's
smelly feet,

Sniff
Sniff

and he tried to
push the dog away
and his other foot got
stuck to the dog,

and now he's waiting
for the fire brigade
to come and
rescue him.

It's 3.37.

23

Perhaps he came home from school
and thought the goldfishes
looked cold,

and poured boiling water into the
fishbowl to warm them up, and
killed them all,

and his mother might have been
angry with him for being such a
twit, and made him
weed the garden,

and de-flea the dog,

and wash the
budgie's hair,

and clean
the inside of
the toilet bowl
with his bare
hands,

and won't let him go out for a week.

It's 3.38.

Perhaps a tiger escaped from a
circus and chased him,

and he ran away and hid in a dustbin,

and the dustbin men came along
and tipped him into the back of
their truck,

and he got scrunched up in all the
rotten smelly garbage,

and tipped out
on to the town
rubbish tip.

It's 3.39.

Perhaps he got caught by that old witch who lives at number twenty-three.

Perhaps she hooked her walking stick in the back of his trousers

as he walked past her house on the way to meet me,

and she
put a spell
on him, and
turned him into
a toad,

and gave him to the
cat to play with.

Perhaps he was trying to cross the road, and some demonstrators were coming,

and he got caught up and
carried along against his will,

and when the demonstrators were
chased by the police, he got bonked
on the head, and bundled into
a police van, and carted off to prison,

EE·AW·EE·AW·EE·AW·EE·

and locked in an overcrowded cell
with four fierce villains, and only
three beds – and the warder's lost
the key.

It's 3.41.

Perhaps he was on
his way to meet me
and a flying saucer
landed in the road, and some weird
luminous creatures got out and
kidnapped him

and carried him
off to their planet in
space, and they're going to keep him
in a zoo, and all the funny space
monsters will pay their pocket
money to come to look at him,
and laugh.

EARTHLING
PATHETICUS

It's 3.42.

Perhaps he was watching TV

and something in the television programme reached out of the screen and got hold of him

and dragged him in, so now he's a
prisoner in a TV show and
can't get out,

and if he did get out
he'd be so small,

his mother
wouldn't
see him,

and when she was
cleaning the carpet

she'd hoover him up,

Darren?

and no one would
ever know where
he went.

It's 3.43.

Perhaps he got lost, and ended up at
the airport by mistake,

and some hijackers
came along and took
poor Darren hostage,
and stole an aeroplane,

and after they'd taken off, a hand
grenade rolled under his seat,
and he wondered what the pin was
for, and pulled it out,

and it blew a great big hole in
the floor,

and he

fell

through –

and now, he might be

stranded

on a

lonely

mountainside,

hanging

upside

down

by his ankles

in a tree.

It's 3.44.

Perhaps, when he was hurrying
along, with his heart pounding in
his chest with the anticipation of
seeing me,

there was an earthquake, and the

ground opened up beneath his feet,
and he fell into the crevice,

like a filling in a sandwich,

and the earth closed up again

and made him as flat as a piece
of greasy beef in a hamburger,
and all his insides squirted out of
the top of his head like a
rainbow-coloured fountain,

and it will be on the front page of the newspaper, and there'll be a photo of me, because I'm his girlfriend, and our names rhyme.

The Daily Trumpet

BOY SQUASHED IN EARTHQUAKE HORROR!

Heroine waits in vain.

Today, a violent earth tremor tragically swallowed up poor ten-year-old Darren White. His girlfriend the beautiful and celebrated Sharon Green, waited for him at a corner shop in town, never guessing the horror that had befallen the boy she loved. "It couldn't have happened to a nicer person," she said, with tears filling her gorgeous eyes, while photographers from all over the world queued to take her picture, and journalists from every continent clamoured for appointments to ... her.

Sharon Green... "I waited."

the fame and wealth that await her, she will never forget the boy she once loved who sacrificed his life in a gallant endeavour to be at her side during yesterday's ... ter.

gedy. E es told crevice in the Darr inte of t ... the

It's 3.45.

I'm going home.

I wouldn't want to be *his* girlfriend – that Darren. He does things under his desk in class when teacher isn't looking!

I'm going
to call for
Michael Breen.

He might buy
me a crunchy bar.

Michael Breen and Sharon Green —

we make a poem!